TO ALL MY WELL WISHERS

Contents

Preface — vii

1. Laugh It Off — 1
2. The Will Divine — 2
3. The Secret Of Success — 4
4. He Had Fixed His Goal — 5
5. Work For The Love Of God — 6
6. We Are Always Late — 7
7. Dethrone The Ego — 8
8. Appreciate! Appreciate! — 10
9. Safe Landing — 12
10. Two Of A Kind — 13
11. My Treasure Is In Heaven — 14
12. God Never Sleeps — 15
13. Taken For Granted — 17
14. The Best Legacy — 18
15. Forgive And Forgotten — 20
16. Not A Laughing Matter — 21
17. Miracle Of Love — 22
18. Two Makes You Happy, Three Robs You Of It — 23
19. Oak Or Squash — 24
20. Never Take Offence — 25
21. The Power That Is God — 26
22. Sensitive As An Opal — 28
23. The True Art Of Living — 29

Contents

24.	The Greatest Attitude	31
25.	Conservation Of The Life Force	32
26.	Chapter 26	34
27.	Command To The Lord	35
28.	Forgive Me My Lord	36
29.	Worship Of God	37
30.	Grace Of God	39
31.	Paths Of Advancement And Degradation	40
32.	Self Or God Realisation	41

Preface

A number of people attack a disciple of a great master, some spit at him, some beat him, some pelt stones at him, some tear his clothes, and some abuse him. He continues to smile.

A man says to him, "where is your master? Why does he not appear in this hour of your piteous need and show us a miracle.

Quietly answers the disciple, "What greater miracle than this that even though I am treated thus, I feel I am in Heaven?"

Astonished, the man asks, " I find you are being treated as though you were in Hell! Where is your Heaven?"

The disciple smiles again and again and says, " My Heaven is within my heart; and no man may take it away from me. Even if my body is cut into pieces; yet will I continue to abide in the joy that is deathless".

The man asks what is the secret of your joy?" The disciple answers," I bow to the Will Divine. In His Will is my highest good. For the Lord loves me and i love Him!

CHAPTER ONE

Laugh It Off

In the event of a provoking situation, look at the humour in it and laugh it off. It will lighten the moment and ease off the tension.

A man from the neighbouring village had came to Mullah Nasruddin's house to have a discussion with him. Since they had decided the data and time of the meet previously, the man scribbed, IDIOTIC DUNCE on the Mullah's door.

When the Mullah returned he read the words on the door and immediately went to the man's house in the neighbouring village and knocked on the door. He apologized to the man and said, " I am sorry that I didnot remember you were coming. But I realised you had come the moment I saw your ignorance on the door".

Moral:- We are the masters of the unsaid words, but slaves of these we let slop out.

CHAPTER TWO

The Will Divine

A number of people attack a disciple of a great master, some spit at him, some beat him, some pelt stones at him, some tear his clothes, and some abuse him. He continues to smile.

A man says to him, "where is your master? Why does he not appear in this hour of your piteous need and show us a miracle.

Quietly answers the disciple, "What greater miracle than this that even though I am treated thus, I feel I am in Heaven?"

Astonished, the man asks, " I find you are being treated as though you were in Hell! Where is your Heaven?"

The disciple smiles again and again and says, " My Heaven is within my heart; and no man may take it away from me. Even if my body is cut into pieces; yet will I continue to abide in the joy that is deathless".

The man asks what is the secret of your joy?" The disciple answers," I bow to the Will Divine. In His Will is my highest good. For the Lord loves me and i love Him!

Yes, the man who bows to the Will Divine, who loves the Lord and lives in Him, knows that all is well, Supremely well! For him Heaven is here and now and forever and evermore!

Moral:- Well sings Atter, the great sufi Saint;
They deem it crime to flee from Destiny,
For Destiny to them brings only Sweetness,
Welcome is all that ever can befall them;
For were it fire, it turns to living waters,
And prison melts to sugar on their lips;
The mire they tread is lustrous diamond,
And weal and woe alike, whatever comes,
They and their kingdom lie in God's
Divineness.

CHAPTER THREE

The Secret Of Success

The Secret Of Success

Hari was a lazy student at the National Engineering College. He was faced with a very difficult exam. So he borrowed all the books on that subject from his library, store them neatly on his book shelf at home and happily announced to his friends, "I am fully prepared for the exam".

His friends were taken aback. They asked him. "How could you be prepared all of a sudden, almost overnight?" And he answered blithely, "I have all the material that I need for the exam".

Borrowing all the books in the library is not adequate preparation for the exam. Only reading them, absorbing their contents will help you pass the test.

Hardwork is the key to success, whether you are a musician or a writer, an athlete or a businessman, the only way you are going to get anywhere in life is by working hard.

Hard work keeps your dreams alive!

Moral:- Laziness may appear attractive, but work gives satisfaction.

CHAPTER FOUR

He Had Fixed His Goal

When Abraham Lincoln was a young boy, he worked as a farm labourer, doing heavy, manual work for three days so that he could earn a little money, to pay for a second hand copy of the life of "Washington". He read the book avidly, and said to an acquaintance, Mrs. Crawford. " I shall be the President" announced Abraham Lincoln. I don't intend to do this, you know--- delve, grab, husk corn, split rails and the like.

What do you want to be then? Asked Mrs. Crawford. "I shall be the President", announced Abraham Lincoln. " I shall study and get ready and the chance will come".

The chance came and Abraham lincoln was ready to take on the most powerful position in the land--- for he had fixed his goal early.

It has been said that winners make goals, while losers make excuses.

Moral:-- Arise! Awake! And stop not till the goal is reached.

CHAPTER FIVE

Work For The Love Of God

On the upper galleries of the cathedral of Milan, there are many statues of Saints carved in exquisite white marble. The dedicated sculptor who created these masterpieces was busy at his work when one of his friends came to see him.

I don't see why you are wasting your artistic effort in such a place. High up here, in these unseen galleries, nobody will ever get to look at your statues. Therefore, your work will not really be appreciated. Isn't that a pity?

It is enough for me that you recognize their value, smiled the artist.

And what if I had not climbed up all those stairs to see your work? Countered the friend.

"My friend", said the artist, "Surely God and His angels would have seen it, and that is enough.

Moral:-- Whatever you do, always think of God. Work not for wages, but for the love of God.

CHAPTER SIX

We Are Always Late

Aristotle was the most respected teacher in Athens. The city's best and brightest young men gathered around him at his Lyccum to receive an allround "Liberal" education, aimed at making them ideal citizens and ideal human beings.

Once, a young mother approached Aristotle she dreamt of the day when her little son would become Aristotle's student.

In her eagerness she wanted the boy to be prepared for it right from his childhood.

"When should I begin training my child, so that he may grow up to be an ideal human being?" she asked the great teacher.

"How old is your child?" enquired Aristotle.

"He is barely five now," said the eager mother.

"Waste no more time", dear lady " said Aristotle, "You are already five years late".

Begin with the womb. If the seed is well nurtured, it will grow into a healthy and strong sapling.

Moral:-- Free the child's potential, and you will transform him into the world.

CHAPTER SEVEN

Dethrone The Ego

Once a great King decided to renounce his power and possessions and seek initiation from Gautam Buddha to become a monk. The entire assembly of bhikkus had gathered around the hermitage to witness this royal initiation ceremony.

The King arrived, dressed in an ochre robe. His head was shaven and he had dispensed with all his ornaments. He walked with bare feet through the assembly of monks-- and in his right hand, he carried a priceless diamond, as an offering to the Master. In his left hand, he carried a rare and beautiful white lotus-- in case of the Buddha refused to accept the ostentations offering of the diamond.

Buddha seated with closed eyes, said to the King, "Drop it!"

The King, was aware of the unsuitability of the offering, immediately dropped the diamond. Buddha's voice commanded again, "Drop it!"

This time the King dropped the lotus.

Again the voice commanded, "Drop it".

The king baffled, for he had nothing to drop now. He continued to walk towards the Master. But the Buddha said once again, "I say to you, drop it!"

The king understand. In one of Buddha's discourses, he had heard the Master say, "Yena tyajasi tam tyaja"---leave that (the ego or the I thought) through which you have left everything!

He understood that he was still in the grip of the ego; he was still entertaining the thought that he had dropped the diamond and lotus at the Lakshmi, your beauty and charm are irresistible when you walk towards me!

With wisdom, you can find a solution to every problem.

Moral:- Wisdom outweighs any wealth.

CHAPTER EIGHT

Appreciate! Appreciate!

A survey of women in rural America revealed that farmer's wives had one common complaint; they were taken for granted. They were hardly ever thanked for what they did.

One of them narrated an amusing incident. Everyday she took the trouble to make a delicious meal to set before her husband and sons when they returned home from work in the evening. She learnt new recipes she prepared complicated dishes. It is obvious that they enjoyed the meal for they gobbled the food down so fast that it disappeared in no time at all. But not a word of thanks, not a single compliment was ever given.

In exasperation one evening, the mother made a meal of cattle feed and set it, steaming hot, on the table. Down they swooped on the food.

"What is this?" They screamed, when they had downed the first mouthful, "Are you crazy or what?"

I have united 26 years and not heard a word of praise from you, she replied. "I never ever thought that you would notice the difference."

Moral:-- Appreciate is a wonderful thing. It makes what is excellent in others belong to us as well.

SUNIL SACHWANI

CHAPTER NINE

Safe Landing

A little boy was trapped on the first floor of a burning house. He had climbed on the ledge of a window to escape the flames, and hung precariously on to the window sill. He was beside himself with terror clinging on for dear life to the window, unable to look up or down.

A strong neighbour came below the window and shouted to him, "Drop down Raju, and I will catch you!"

On hearing this, the boy just let go and fell safely into the big man's arms. "I knew you would catch me uncle", he said gratefully, putting his arms around the man's neck.

All we have to do is trust God-- and all will be well!

Moral:-- Trust in the the Lord with all your heart; and lean not upon your own understanding. In all your ways acknowledge him, and he shall direct your path.

CHAPTER TEN

Two Of A Kind

A little boy was holding a sparrow with a broken wing. A kind lady saw him sitting solemnly on the pook bench, stroking the wounded bird.

" Sorry, would you like me to take this sparrow home and nurse it back to good health?" She asked him gently.

She assumed that the boy was feeling sorry for the bird, but didn't know what to do with it.

"I promise you, I will bring it back here when it is headed," she continued, "Together we will let it free again."

The little boy thought for a moment. Then he said to her, "Thank you madam, but I would like to take care of the bird myself".

He paused and then added, "You see, I can understand this bird better".

The lady was about to protest, when she saw the boy rise up. Then she realised that the boy was lame. His left leg was in a caliper.

Even sympathy follows the law of attraction.

Moral:- The great gift of human beings is that we have the power of empathy.

CHAPTER ELEVEN

My Treasure Is In Heaven

A kind and compassionate Emperor distribute vast qualities of his wealth among the poor in a year of famine.

His brothers said to him, "Our father and forefathers gathered these treasures over several generations, each adding to those of his father. You are giving away our wealth and theirs! You will surely live to rue this!"

The King said to them, "My forefathers gathered treasures of money-- I have gathered treasures in souls.

"My father gathered treasures for earth-- I have gathered treasures for heaven.

"My father gathered treasures for others-- I have gathered treasures for myself."

Truly has it been said, charity is a virtue of the heart and not the hand.

Moral:- Greatness lies not in trying to be somebody but in trying to help somebody.

CHAPTER TWELVE

God Never Sleeps

Little Tina, all of four years old, was spending the weekend with her grandmother. They were happily watching television at night, when a thunderstorm broke out, and the electric supply was cut off. Their little flat was plunged into darkness.

I think we should go to bed now, said the grandmother after sometime. It's nearly ten O'clock now.

"Its so dark, and I am afraid," whispered little Tina.

"That's easily set right", said the grandmother, cheerfully drawing open the curtains of the bedroom window. The child caught a glimpse of the moon in the sky.

Our lights may be off, said the lady. "But you can see God's light is on!"

Grandma, said the child, "is the moon God's own light.

"Of course it is!"

The next question was, "won't God put out His light and go to sleep?"

"No honey." smiled the grandmother."God never goes to sleep?"

In her simple and beautiful faith, the child said, " well, as long as God is awake I am not afraid!"

Moral:- When I walk by the wayside, he is along with me. When i enter into company amid all my forgetfulness of Him, He never forgets me. In the silent watches of the night, when my eyelids are closed and my spirit has sunk into unconsciousness, the observant eye of Him who never slumbers is upon me.

CHAPTER THIRTEEN

Taken For Granted

Of a great english poet, i read that he wrote poems and dedicated them to the famous and wealthy. Also haughty and selfish. At home he never spoke a word of love or appreciation to his wife. So long as she lived, he criticised her and found fault with everything that she did. Suddenly, the wife died. The poet was grief-stricken. He was ashamed that he had failed to write poems in appreciation of her when she had been alive. " If only I had known" he lamented. 'If only I had known".

Truly has it been said the life is too short to be small. Let us not be small-minded. Let us be generous with praise, appreciation and encouragement.

Moral:- The greatest weakness of most humans is their hesitancy to tell others how much they love them while they're still alive.

CHAPTER FOURTEEN

The Best Legacy

A rich businessman came to seek his Guru's advice on a matter that had been bothering him.

"I have amassed a fortune for my sons," he said to the sage. "My problem `is that i do not know what is the best and safe manner to invest it for my children. Gold is not reliable; stocks and shares fluctuate wildly; real estate does not always pay good returns. What shall I do? Where shall I put my money?

"Give your children the kind of wealth that no one can take away from them", the sage advised him. "Give them the wealth of good education and good up bringing filled with values and ideals.

Research had proven that the world's wealthiest are not necessarily the world's happiest.

However, the lives of countless great men of humanity have proven that happiness stems forth from within. It is essentially an inner feeling.

Moral:-- Most people say that is it is the intellect which makes a great scientist. They are wrong; it is character.

SUNIL SACHWANI

CHAPTER FIFTEEN

Forgive And Forgotten

A young girl called Priya, grew so much in the love of God, that she was actually able to commune with Sri Krishna her ishta.

A doubting faithless priest to put her to the test, " As if you claim, you really commune with Sri Krishna everyday, ask Him to tell you what was the sin I continued to committed when I was a young man.

He was sure that she would never find out. And this would expose her claim as being false.

Next week, he sought her out and asked her, " Have you spoken to Sri krishna?"

"Yes, i did," she replied.

And did he tell you what was the sin I committed.?"

"He told me that He had forgotten it--and wanted you to do the same".

The doubting priest hung his head in shame.

"If God does not keep a tally of people's faults and failings, why should we?"

Moral:-- No one is perfect......that's why pencils have erasers.

CHAPTER SIXTEEN

Not A Laughing Matter

Two men who served in the second World War were severely injured. Each had to have an arm amputated. They were both sent to a rehabilitation centre for the disabled, where they underwent training to use their one arm as efficiently as possible.

At the end of one year's training, one of them was so discouraged that he came to the conclusion that life was not worth living with such a handicap as he had.

The other soldier was so happy with the training, he had received, that he went about telling everyone. It is a boon that God has given people two arms, where we can get along perfectly well with just one!"

That man was indeed an optimist!

Moral:-- For despair, optimism is the only practical solution. Hope is always practical.

CHAPTER SEVENTEEN

Miracle Of Love

There was a man who led an evil life, he drank and gambled, and he ill--treated his wife. His wife and children sought comfort at Sadhu Vaswani's Satsang. He did not happen of this.

One day, the man came to Sadhu Vaswani and shook his fist at him and said, "it only you knew how much I hate you!"

Sadhu Vaswani looked lovingly at the man and said to him, "if only you knew how much I love you!

What was there in Sadhu Vaswani's word's? The man came and fell at his feet and with tears in his eyes, begged forgiveness. His life was changed. He turned away from his evil ways. He accompanied his wife and children every evening to the satsang.

Moral:-- Darkness cannot drive out darkness; only light can do that. Hate cannot drive out hate; only love can do that.

CHAPTER EIGHTEEN

Two Makes You Happy, Three Robs You Of It

One day, Benjamin Franklin, an American philosopher, called out to his little son and gave him an apple.

The boy was very happy to receive the apple. His eyes sparkled with joy.

Benjamin gave him another apple and the boy took it in his other hand. Now, both his little hands were filled with juicy red apples.

Benjamin then gave him a third apple the child was overwhelmed with joy, but as he tried to hold the third apple, all the three apples fell to the ground. The child began to cry.

Despite having everything, man continues to crave for more. And it is this craving that is the cause of our happiness.

Moral:- He who is not contentment with what he has, would not be contented with what he would like to have.

CHAPTER NINETEEN

Oak Or Squash

To meet James Garfield at Hiram College, came a rich and haughty gentleman, accompanied by his son who was an undergraduate.

Look here, Mr. Garfield, my son is very happy to be here in your college. But does his degree programme really have to last three whole years? Can't you shorten the courses so that he might pass out sooner? I can't wait to get my dreams fulfilled through him."

"It all depends on what you want out of his education," Garfield replied quietly, "Even God takes a hundred years to make an oak tree; but a squash takes just two months."

There are no shortcuts to good things.

Moral:- When it comes to success, there are no shortcuts!

CHAPTER TWENTY

Never Take Offence

Uday singh had a Bachelor's degree in commerce but no job. Desperate to earn a livelihood he managed to borrow a meagre sum of money. Finally, he put up a small shop with sundry garments.

On the first day, a wealthy woman walked in and complained. "This place has nothing but bits and pieces and walked out. Uday did not take offence or get angry, in fact he thanked her and the next day put up a board outside the shop saying 'Bits and Pieces".

He began to flourish selling miscellaneous items.

If we look at the things with a new and positive perspective--we will benefit immediately or immensely.

Moral:-- A pessimist sees the difficulty in every opportunity; an optimist sees the opportunity in every difficulty.

CHAPTER TWENTY-ONE

The Power That Is God

There was a villager who was invited to visit his rich cousin, who lived in a city. The villager was amazed by the gadgets and electronic marvels that filled his cousin's house. He hit the heights of amazement when he was whisked off to the fifteenth floor office of his cousin in an elevator.

"This is unbelievable! This is miraculous!" Exclaimed the villager. Truly, cousin, you are great, why you have made us go up at the touch of a button!

As they neared the fourteenth floor, there was a power failure. The elevator came to a standstill, and the lights blacked out.

"Can't you do something?" the villager asked in panic. His rich cousin had to admit that it was actually the electricity which made all the "marvels" possible. On his own, he could do nothing without its power.

So it is with the body; it is the soul within us which is eternal, everlasting. The body is physical, material, phenomenal, destructible; when the atman goes, the body drops down dead.

Moral:-- The soul can never be cut into pieces by any weapon, nor burned by and fire-- nor moistened by water, nor withered by the wind.

SUNIL SACHWANI

CHAPTER TWENTY-TWO

Sensitive As An Opal

A tourist was looking at the display in a famous Delhi Jewellery store. Exquisite emeralds, rubies and diamonds dazzled the eye. But his attention was drawn to a dull stone, completely lacking in lustre

"That's certainly not as beautiful as the rest", he exclaimed.

"Just a moment", said the jeweller, taking the stone from the tray and closing his palms around it.

Moments later he opened his palm and the stone glowed with beauty. "This is an opal", the jeweller explained, "Its what we call a sensitive jewel. It needs only to be held with a human hand to bring out its radiance and lustrous beauty.

Doesn't this strike a parallel to emotions that we share with people around us? The warmth affection and love we give to them brings out the beauty in all human relations and leaves us beaming and radiant with joy.

Moral:-- affection is responsible for nine--tenths of whatever solid and durable happiness there is in our lives.

CHAPTER TWENTY-THREE

The True Art Of Living

There was a distinguished painter whose works were highly sought after by millionaire. A business executive was flying long distance across the Pacific. A little boy travelling home for his holidays was seated next to him. As the passengers were dozing after an excellent lunch, there was an urgent message from the pilot to fasten their seat-belts, as the plane was about to run into stormy weather, heavy rain and wind. Despite the enormous size of the plane and the power of its engines, the flight was jolted badly.

The boy became desperately afraid and clung to the older man's arms. For his part, the man strokes the boy's head gently to reassure him.

Aren't you afraid? Whispered the boy, as the plane dipped all of a sudden.

No! Laughed the man. "This is real fun, isn't it? Aren't you enjoying yourself?

An immediate change came over the little boy. His fear and tension left him and he too, began to enjoy the "fun", laughing and squealing delightedly as the plane dipped and swayed.

The executive had taught the young one a valuable lesson in the art of living.

Moral:-- Life is 10% what happens to you and 90% how you react to it.

CHAPTER TWENTY-FOUR

The Greatest Attitude

There was a distinguished painter whose works were highly sought after by millionaire art-collectors. One day, somebody broke into his studio and stole his latest masterpiece. The painter shrugged off the incident. When his friends arrived to express their regrets the following day, they found him relaxing in his garden, much as usual.

How could you be so cool and unconcerned? They asked him. That painting of yours which was stolen has probably set you back by a million dollars!

You have lost a fortune and his friend, the banker. You are mistaken, said the painter," One of my pictures was stolen. But that was not my fortune. My real fortune is right here! And he painted to his head. This is my true fortune which helped me produce all my pictures. And there are many more pictures waiting to be produced there!

Positive attitude is the greatest fortune one can possess.

Moral:- Attitude is a little thing that makes a big difference.

CHAPTER TWENTY-FIVE

Conservation Of The Life Force

You are going somewhere, and on the way you happen to see a carcass or someone's vomit or excreta. At that time revulsion develops in your mind whereupon a fraction of your life--force diminishes.

What should be done at such a point? The Saints suggest that one should remember and have darshan of either the Sun God (a mere glance is enough), the Fire God, a deity the pinnacle of a temple, or chant the holy name of the Lord. This prevents the precious life-force from diminishing. One should avoid urinating while facing the Sun, as this may create certain complications like headache etc. in future.

Irrespective of how rich our dietary intake is or how diligently we do our japa, if we do not pay head to such minor points in life, we become prone to losing our vital force. Infact, we lose the ability to make proper use of our life-force, and exercise restraint on the mind and senses when such a need arises.

SUNIL SACHWANI

CHAPTER TWENTY-SIX

May Good Prevail In Everyone's Life

If your mind harbours ill feeling towards somebody; it may or may not afflict them but your own antahkarana certainly becomes vitiated in the process. This gives rise to restlessness, which is the root cause of all miseries and sufferings.

Suppose your mind harbours malice towards some one. It would be better to approach that person and plead, "please pardon me" whenever I see you a feeling of malice overpowers my mind. "Please pray for me and I will pray too so that this ill feeling gets eradicated!"

No matter has intently one is determined to harm you, if you remain cautious and nurture good feelings towards them and wish for their good alone, then no one can cause you any harm. Your positive attitude will transform their negative thoughts and their harmful intentions will never come to fruition.

CHAPTER TWENTY-SEVEN

Command To The Lord

Those who cavilling at My teaching do not practise it, deluded in wisdom, devoid of discrimination, senseless are doomed.

With your mind fixed on me, you shall overcome all difficulties by My Grace. If you will not listen to me, you shall perish.

Never is this to be spoken by you to one who is devoid of austerities or devotion, nor to one who does not render service or who does not desire to listen, nor to one who cavils at me.

However, he who with Supreme devotion to me, will teach this Supreme secret to My devotees, shall come to Me.

Be devoted to Me, worship Me, you shall come to Me only. Truly this is My promise.

Fix your mind on Me, be devoted to Me, adore Me, and make obeisance to Me you shall come to Me.

CHAPTER TWENTY-EIGHT

Forgive Me My Lord

Bowing down and prostrating before you. Adorable Lord I seek Your Grace, Forgive me, O Lord, as a father forgives his son, as a friend his friend, and as a lover his beloved.

You are the Prime Deity, the most ancient Person. You are the Ultimate Resort, the knower and the knowable. It is you by whom the Universe pervaded. O one of infinite forms.

You are the creator of this world and father of Brahma and greatest Guru. you are to be worshipped; there is none equal to you in the three worlds, O Being of incomparable unequalled Power.

You know Yourself by Yourself, O Lord, source of beings. Lords, the Gods of gods, O Lord of the world. Salutation! Salutation! Salutation to you, my Lord.

CHAPTER TWENTY-NINE

Worship Of God

Believing in God, is worship of God
Forgiveness is worship of God
Loving others is worship of God
Rendering selfless service is worship of God
Duty performed as an offering is worship Of God.
Reading, reciting and teaching Gita is Worship of God
Adoring creation is worship of God
Practicing good code of conduct is Worship of God
Abiding in His will is worship of God
Giving gifts for worthy cause is worship Of God
To see the same lord in all and all in Him is worship of God
Surrendering to the God is worship of God .

CHAPTER THIRTY

Grace Of God

I give heat. I send rain. I stop rain. I support and sustain the entire universe.

Rain produces food. Food produces beings. I secure my devotees what they do not possess and take care of what they already possess.

I am the origin of all. I am the beginning of the Universe. I am the end of the Universe.

Whatever being has power, glory or energy, know to be born of a part of My Splendour.

God bestows Divine love and protection freely upon mankind. He renders mercy even upon people who do not deserve it.

Out of compassion for my devotees. I dwelling in their self, destroy the darkness born of ignorance by the shining light of wisdom.

CHAPTER THIRTY-ONE

Paths Of Advancement And Degradation

Our soul can be our friend or foe. It all depends upon our deeds, both in thought and action.

The cruel haters, worst among the men in the world I hurl them into the wombs of demons only.

At the time of death, whatsoever the person thinks of, that alone he attains because of his constant thought of that being.

And he who departs from the body, remember me alone at the time of death he attains my being; there is no doubt about this.

Therefore, at all times remember the Lord with mind and intellect absorbed in Him, you shall without doubt go to Him.

CHAPTER THIRTY-TWO

Self Or God Realisation

Self Or God Realisation

Knowledge of soul (spirit) cannot be attained simply by reading scriptures and listening to religious discourses. Through yoga of wisdom you experience that there are two purusa in you, body and soul.

The moment of self- realisation comes up when you are ready to receive it, you are pure and truthful. You will feel physically unwell but still you will feel happy and well in your heart.

Yoga of wisdom leads you to God-- realisation when you realise that all this creation is nothing but Vasudeva (God).

You have to transcend senses, mind or intellect through recitation of Naam, practice of yoga of meditation and rendering self--less service (Yoga of Action) to attain God realisation.

Knowledge of soul (spirit) cannot be attained simply by reading scriptures and listening to religious discourses. Through yoga of wisdom you experience that there are two purusa in you, body and soul.

The moment of self- realisation comes up when you are ready to receive it, you are pure and truthful. You will feel physically unwell but still you will feel happy and well in your heart.

Yoga of wisdom leads you to God-- realisation when you realise that all this creation is nothing but Vasudeva (God).

You have to transcend senses, mind or intellect through recitation of Naam, practice of yoga of meditation and rendering self--less service (Yoga of Action) to attain God realisation.

ABOUT THE AUTHOR

I(MR. SALIM J ABDULLA) hereby informs you that my friend's son Mr. SUNIL S SACHWANI working as full time Banker and pursues his hobby and flair for writing religious discourses and articles in his spare time . His religious books are of high standards and gives one insight into the Hindu Religion and the standard of material and discourses can match Radha Swami Satsang Beas and other Saint's discourses which I heard many times on television and heard many times in Pune Maharashtra. The undersigned has read many books of high standard, written by many Saints and their disciples. MR. SUNIL S SACHWANI's insight matches them and 'their disciples the reader truly feels enriched with truth and the path of the great Saints. MR. SUNIL S SACHWANI deserves all help and encouragement to continue with his great work, the trails of spiritual life and writings MR. SUNIL S SACHWANI has bequeathed have got from his father, who was a very successful and intellectual Banker. He would feel be proud of him, if he was alive.

As MR. SUNIL S SACHWANI joined BANK OF INDIA in October 1993. As he came to know about BANK OF INDIA's quarterly Magazine "Taarangan" is published by BANK OF INDIA, his first article was published in March 2000, subject was "A POSSITIVE APPROACH TO OLD AGE" I have read his articles since March 2000, were of great success and will be roaring success in the hands of Indian Intellectuals and also to general public. Once I asked MR. SUNIL S SACHWANI about his articles, from where you get tittles of articles. He informed me that these are general topics and we are facing these topics in our everyday life. He informed me that once in my college days, when I was in H.S.C., a Hindi professor kept an essay competition among his class students a girl student has attempted that essay topic so he was teasing other students for challenge to that girl student in 1983. From that day onwards he started writing the articles. He got the first prize on-articles invited by ANDHERI SINDHI PANCHAYAT among members or member's children. MR. SUNIL S SACHWANI has written ten pages (10 pages) on the topic "SECURITY SCAM." From that day onwards he started writing articles whole heartedly. After his marriage in 1994, when he saw his Father-In-Law who was working in WESTERN RAILWAY MUMBAI HEAD QUARTERS, was writings books in his mother tongue i.e. SINDHI language on full scale. So this boosted his confidence to write books in English or HINDI. From that day onwards he tried to write books on various Religious topics. While he got success in writing articles, sometimes poems or books depend on his mood.

I wish MR. SUNIL S SACHWANI who deserves all encouragement and support from all of us to write the books on various religious topics. I wish him to get roaring success in that field through the blessings of all of us and by general public and also godly person's i.e. Saints. My best wishes to a very interesting author.

With regards

MR. SALIM J ABDULLA

Biography of author

The Author Mr. Sunil Sachwani, was born in April 1964 and is a Mumbai resident, professionally he is a banker in free time after banking hours he spends time in performing various duties such as household work and writing articles and books.

He writes articles for his Bank's magazine called "Taarangan" which is published by Bank of India quarterly for the staff of the Bank of India. In 1995 he was inspired by his father-in-law, who as a senior citizen used to write books.

The author has written three books in a period of 8-9 days of privilege leave. The author possesses the ability of how to utilize the spare time! So, this is one such example keeping busy in his daily life.

www.ingramcontent.com/pod-product-compliance
Lightning Source LLC
LaVergne TN
LVHW041547060526
838200LV00037B/1186